D1248797

Old Dog

GROUNDWOOD BOOKS
HOUSE OF ANANSI PRESS
TORONTO   BERKELEY

Old Dog

Teresa Cárdenas

Translated by David Unger

Groundwood Books / House of Anansi Press
110 Spadina Avenue, Suite 801, Toronto, Ontario M5V 2K4

Distributed in the USA by Publishers Group West
1700 Fourth Street, Berkeley, CA 94710

We acknowledge for their financial support of our publishing
program the Government of Canada through the Book Publishing
Industry Development Program (BPIDP).

Library and Archives Canada Cataloguing in Publication
Cárdenas, Teresa
Old dog / by Teresa Cárdenas; translated by David Unger.
Translation of: Perro viejo.
ISBN-13: 978-0-88899-757-9 (bound) –
ISBN-10: 0-88899-757-4 (bound)
ISBN-13: 978-0-88899-836-1 (pbk.) –
ISBN-10: 0-88899-836-8 (pbk.)
1. Unger, David II. Title.
PZ7C196O1 2007   j863'.64   C2005-903214-1-0

Cover image: *Harper's New Monthly Magazine* (January 1853), vol. 6,
p.169. Special Collections Department, University of Virginia Library.

Design by Michael Solomon
Printed and bound in Canada

For Susy and Felipe
In memory of Zenita

Mountain Coffee

Perro Viejo brought the rim of the cup up to his nose and sniffed. The aroma of coffee sweetened with honey wafted into his nostrils, comforting him.

He always smelled things first. It was a habit, something learned over the years. He brought his lips together and took a sip. The coffee slid down his throat like a warm stream, all the way to his stomach.

"Bless you, Beira!" he mumbled happily.

At the rear of the shack, a strong woman moved nimbly about, separating the blackened pitchers from the pots. The wood burning in the fire crackled in front of her.

As he watched her, Perro Viejo realized that the quiet and sometimes clumsy woman made better coffee — aromatic, bitter, wild, free mountain coffee — than anyone else on the sugar plantation.

Perro Viejo stopped drinking. "Mountain coffee?" he asked, not understanding the meaning of the words spinning in his head.

He put the cup down on the table and hobbled to the door.

It was nearly pitch black outside. A few pale stars flickered in the dark, moonless sky. A cold wind blew through the bushes and the yagruma trees near the front gate.

Perro Viejo shuddered. It was four in the morning. The dogs in the courtyard started barking. With great effort, he sat down on a low stool and focused his cloudy eyes on the shadows and silhouettes dragging hoes and machetes past the door of his shack.

"Coffee from which mountain?" he asked himself, making a sour face.

He had never climbed a mountain. In fact, he had no idea where the dusty road that began beyond the rows of gum and flamboyant trees led. Never in his life had he been beyond the plantation gate. He was seventy years old and had no memory of living elsewhere.

Perro Viejo closed his eyes and breathed softly. Beira was humming in a strange language at the other end of the shack.

Far off a whip cracked, the sound nearly lost among the barks of the dogs.

Beira

"Do you want more coffee?" she asked in a harsh, hoarse voice.

Startled, Perro Viejo turned around.

Beira was staring at him, her eyes nearly looking right through him. She had the cup he had put down on the table in one hand and a small, steaming pitcher in the other. Her face was as wide and empty as a cane field after being slashed and burned. She wore a shapeless sackcloth dress with no pockets. She was barefoot and had no kerchief covering her hair.

Perro Viejo remembered what the farmhands said about her, but he didn't believe in supernatural things, not at his age. Through the course of his life he had learned not to expect too much from the other world, where he imagined gods and the souls of his ancestors lived.

"Everything that happens on earth, good or bad, is in the hands of the people and in no one else's," he told the farmhands one night. Still, Cumbá, Eulogio Malembe and the others went on blaming evil spirits for the woman's weird doings.

Perro Viejo knew that fire burned. One arm had been so badly charred in the fire that killed old Aroni, Mos and the cook, Micaela Lucumí, that it was almost useless. This had happened thirty years ago and his flesh still smarted.

He shook his head vigorously. Sometimes a hard shake would loosen the memories that hurt him the most.

The fire was going out. The water stopped boiling in the pot. Smoke invaded the room.

"Are you going to drink it or not? I've got things to do," Beira said impatiently.

Perro Viejo shifted restlessly on his stool. He had completely forgotten about her. Lately he was forgetting lots of things.

"It's a cold night," he said just to say something, and he took the cup. While Beira poured a stream of coffee into it, Perro Viejo stared at her hand. It was dark and silky, perhaps a bit too soft for a slave's hand. Fine furrows ran over her knuckles, leaving a strange, rough pattern on her fingers.

Perro Viejo felt Beira's hand brushing his. It

was as cool as the river water he dove into as a child. There was no way those hands had removed pots and pans from the fire without a potholder — no matter what the farmhands said. They also claimed she could jump through flames without burning up and even swallow fire. And when the bosses went to sleep, she was rumored to fly over the plantation in a huge pot that sent sparks into the night as it brushed against the treetops. Surely they were just imagining things.

"What stupid men," he said aloud, without realizing it.

"What did you say, Taita?" Beira asked. She was working busily at the rear of the shack.

Smiling slightly, Perro Viejo turned to her with the idea of telling her what the farmhands said about her.

But he couldn't bring himself to do it.

Beira was leaning over the fire, trying to sweep the remaining kindling together. Red coals danced playfully in her hands.

Beyond the Path

Perro Viejo had no idea what awaited him beyond death. To be honest, he didn't even care.

Sometimes he recalled what Father Andrés said about hell — that it was eternal fire and other such things — and he felt nervous, full of doubts and questions. Not because he thought his soul would burn up for not having obeyed his master, as they assured him it would, but because he knew a lot about fire and what it could do.

Perro Viejo didn't fear hell — he had lived his whole life in it.

On the contrary, the old slave actually liked to imagine his own death.

Very often, he'd close his eyes so that the pictures in his imagination would be sharp. He would see himself dressed in a strangely white linen suit, with a shiny gold pocket watch dangling from his vest. He'd be enjoying the late afternoon breeze on the terrace of the main house, sitting in the boss's easy chair while the boss or his wife served him coffee in a crystal goblet.

At other times, he saw his soul — his spirit or whatever it was called — floating above the plantation gate and the row of yagruma trees before it vanished along the dusty road which, most certainly, led to a life less difficult than his own. Or perhaps the road wasn't the way to heaven or hell, but a direct route to Africa, the land of jungles and plains, where his mother was born.

Perro Viejo snorted, shaking his head to scare off whatever was bothering him.

How many more years of life did he have? Three, four, five? An eternity? It was hard to know for sure. Slaves were born with death inside them and at times it appeared in a surprising way. Perhaps death wouldn't show up as quickly as he might want, or it would come along when he least expected it.

Perro Viejo remembered Nsasi, the little five-year-old boy who was struck and killed by a bullet when the boss's son was cleaning his rifle.

Nsasi was feeding the chickens when he collapsed onto a heap of corn kernels. He stopped breathing. His eyes stayed open as if someone had snatched something out of his hands. After all the fuss, the hens went back to pecking the kernels scattered all over Nsasi's clothes and near his cold fingers.

It had happened in a flash. That same night, while Nsasi was being buried, the boss's wife insisted that the little boy's mother be given a new outfit so she would stop wailing.

What happened to Tumba Cerrada, the conga player, was another story. He was almost one hundred and still walked sprightly and upright. Though he didn't use a cane, he wasn't strong enough to work in the fields. He couldn't be a guard either, because he was half-blind and was always falling asleep.

The boss gave the order to throw him out of the farmhouse and not feed him to see if he would die. But Tumba had a strong constitution. He lived for another five years out of spite, eating rosehips as if he were a woodland bird and left-overs that the farmhands secretly gave him. He slept in the open air among the wooden crosses of the cemetery by the old sugar mill. Any old place was fine for him.

He would have survived like that for many more years, but one day he was found dangling from a huge old tree at the rear of the plantation. When the boss heard about this, he insisted that Tumba Cerrada had tired of living.

No one believed him. There was no way Tumba could have strung himself up from such a tall tree. Whenever anyone claimed he had killed himself, Perro Viejo would snort and spit on the dirt floor.

"What a shitty life!" he'd growl, wishing with all his might to go down the road, far beyond what his eyes could see — far beyond where his tired feet could take him. To go as far as he could, away from hell and his master. Far away.

The Lord

As soon as the bells tolled in the morning, the
slaves would bow their heads to the Lord who
hung naked from a cross on one wall of the
farmhouse near the pig's water trough. Then
they would go out into the snake- and scorpion-
filled cane fields to work, having received the
blessings of the parish priest.

They would cut reeds and sugarcane under
the burning sun, afraid of the foreman's whip.

And later, when arnica and vinegar were
applied to their wounds at the health clinic, the
cutters wouldn't let out even a single scream for
fear of disturbing the master's wife as she napped.

At lunchtime, when the master came into the
courtyard of the sugar mill, they all had to lower
their eyes. And if his son decided to go riding in
the fields beyond the plantation, Perro Viejo had
to open the gate with eyes lowered, not uttering
a single word.

To the gatekeeper, all the whites were alike. Whether they carried crosses, canes, arnica, whips, tiny books or a crown of thorns. A slave could never stand proudly before a white man, much less look one in the face.

Slaves knew that masters owned their lives — their master was the lord, the person who determined which slaves deserved to live or die, which were ready to marry, whether their children could stay with them or whether they'd end up being sold as if they were baskets of fruit.

He controlled their lives and their deaths with greater power than God himself and all the saints that the priest spoke about every Sunday.

A slave was nothing more than a foul-smelling piece of meat. A black man was a beast, an animal, an idiot, a thief, a scoundrel, a bag of coal... A single piece of coal.

A gentleman and a black man could never be equal. Perro Viejo knew that. Black men would never whip a child for having filched a piece of bread. He had never seen Cumbá club a man to death or Beira cut off a man's ear or Malongo rape a young girl...

These atrocities were always carried out by the master or the foreman or their white employees.

Catechism

Father Andrés thought of Perro Viejo as his star student in catechism class. On Sundays, when the slaves were gathered together in the courtyard and the priest sermonized about heaven and angels under the glaring sun, the gatekeeper humbly and attentively lowered his head.

Fortunately, the priest could not read his mind. If he could, he would have realized that instead of following the sermon, Perro Viejo had gone back in time to see himself as a young boy crossing his legs on the floor of the farmhouse, quivering as black Aroni's ceremonious voice told him amazing tales of Africa.

Aroni

"Hey, all of you, listen! You're going to be amazed at what I'm about to tell you. I once knew a man who had hair white as ivory and eyes the color of the raging sea…"

Aroni. Word sorceress. Witch of dreams.

She was always telling stories, anywhere, anytime. Her stories were for everyone whether she sat on the ground or on a stool, surrounded by children or grownups. She told stories to blacks and whites, to the living and the dead, to the wind and the cane fields, to the ducks and even to the ants marching up the courtyard wall.

She was neither sane nor insane, neither happy nor sad. She neither cried nor sang. She only told stories, amazing tales she had heard as a young girl in her African village. From her lips sprouted stories of sorcerers and fierce, bewitched creatures, devils and angels, silver and pearly fish, bearded *duendes* and warrior princes who fell into disgrace.

There were times Perro Viejo and the others couldn't understand what she was saying, but still they listened. By her side, they somehow ended up walking down a narrow tunnel that led to an ogre's cave, or they would fly to the moon holding hands with a magical fish. Sometimes they became kings wearing big ten-gallon red hats that flung bolts of lightning. Or they were simply free men and women with long and beautiful roads ahead of them.

Aroni. Her voice, deep and melodious, like a man's. Aroni, spinning yarns under the trees with her arms spread out or telling stories as she leaned on Cumbá, who'd been punished and placed in the stockade. She told stories to the sons of foremen and talked about fire and water, time and death, about other men and a country where everyone could look each other directly in the face.

Poor Aroni. Mother of tales, woman with a barren womb. As a young girl, she took a potion made in the middle of the night from the bark of the guiro and guanine trees to abort the child a foreman had forcibly implanted in her.

The potion left her high and dry forever.

This was the shortest and most terrifying of her stories, the only one she wouldn't share with others.

For Perro Viejo, the old woman was a magical charm. Because she was alive, he knew for sure that his mother had really existed.

Aroni had brought him into this world. She had brought him out of his mother's warm and embracing womb. Aroni had known his mother. They had gazed into each other's eyes and Aroni had heard his mother talk and groan during childbirth. She had dried his mother's tears.

There were times when the old man wanted to turn back the clock, to see things through Aroni's eyes. From that place full of stories and memories, he would see his mother's face and hold it in the light.

But now it was too late. Fire and time had overwhelmed the old storyteller, consuming her and all the memories of Perro Viejo's youth that he had not been able to recover.

Aroni's voice and stories remained in the gate-keeper's mind, but the true story of her life had not ended happily.

Before

Now with death almost upon him, he was the gatekeeper. But when he had been strong, he had cut sugarcane, cleared the fields, transported the sugarcane pulp on the oxcarts. He had also chopped wood, piled up the kindling, fed the furnaces, emptied the sugar vats, greased the sugar mill gears every week, repaired the farmhouse doors, built the stockade…

And earlier, as a young boy, he had carried firewood to the kitchen in the master's house. He had also planted ñame, yams, carrots, bananas, malanga and pumpkins. He had cleaned the pigsty, bathed the horses and given them water to drink. He had repaired oxcarts, disemboweled ducks, chickens and pigs, cleaned the mud from the boots of the master's son…

And when he wasn't even three feet tall, he'd fed the chicks, led the mules hauling sugarcane pulp on oxcarts, shucked corn, picked up the dirty clothes in the main house, woven straps of leather to make the foreman's new whip... And what about the day he was born? Had he worked even then?

Indeed, Perro Viejo believed he had begun working inside his mother's womb.

He'd been a slave even then.

Beatings

The gatekeeper knew much about sadness, the endless sorrow of all his losses, the restless fear that never left him, the threatening odor of torture and death. But he knew absolutely nothing about love.

He doubted that his heart had the strength or the resistance necessary to experience that feeling. Maybe the reason he couldn't feel love was simple — his heart didn't want to.

He was just a boy when his heart had first beat strangely with feeling. Aroni told the story of the poor young man who found a silver fish and took it all the way to the moon to rescue his mother from the claws of the devil. He liked the story so much he could have sworn his heart had become more powerful than the sugar mill just hearing it. At least the beating of his heart sounded almost as loud as the clanking mill.

But as he grew up, he didn't feel it again until

the afternoon the foreman snapped the whip near his head and sent him to the stockade as punishment. He couldn't remember why, maybe for doing some petty thing. A black man didn't have to do anything to be punished. Anyway, his whole body had vibrated like a drum before the first lash fell on his body.

Still the worst thing his heart had witnessed was when he saw Ulundi's body disappear in the cloud of dust behind the horse that was dragging him — it almost flew out of his chest as his eyes followed that cloud.

The old man was sure the vultures had eaten his heart together with his friend's body, since he no longer felt it inside.

At times he'd put his hand on his chest and it was like placing it on a stone. No heartbeat, no sound. There was nothing inside to indicate he was still alive.

He would watch others working under the sun or in the rain, enduring the bug bites, sleeping piled on each other in the farmhouse, and he'd wonder if they felt the same way.

It was then that he doubted that anything greater actually existed. If he couldn't even say there was a heart in his chest, how could he believe that someone lived in heaven?

Each day Perro Viejo understood less how white men thought.

The Sunday after Ulundi was dragged to his death, the priest assured them that what had happened to their friend was proof of divine will. He held the Bible and the cross to Perro Viejo's lips for him to kiss them and ask for forgiveness, but instead Perro Viejo spat at them as if he were flinging a machete.

The priest ran out of the chapel, but he slipped on the mud and broke his leg and two fingers on his right hand.

Perro Viejo was sent to the stockade for a second time and received one hundred lashes for his blasphemy.

The bloody, torn skin on his back seemed to be on fire. He almost died. Nevertheless, he held back his rage breath by breath. He had no choice but to give them his life, but he stubbornly refused to give them his death as well.

Asunción

Perro Viejo never had a chance to find out what affection was. In fact, he didn't even recognize the word.

Yes, he'd been with women in the darkness of the farmhouse, surrounded by the snores of his fellow workers. And in the cane fields or behind the kitchen of the main house.

But he didn't feel the passion he saw in Luciano's eyes, for example, when he watched Keta coming back from the river with a basket of damp clothes on her head. Or Malongo's affection for horses and the other creatures on the plantation. He felt none of the devotion that other men had for the gods that lived and died with them in the farmhouse or the stockade. He certainly had none of the gentleness he saw in Carlota as she planted flowers — the earth itself seemed to welcome her. Her flowers were respected equally by dry spells, floods or the savage wind that blew across the cane fields or the hungry swarm of bees after a hard rain. Her hands seemed to have a magical relationship with nature.

And not even that stirred Perro Viejo's heart.

After Ulundi died, Perro Viejo wanted nothing to do with anything or anyone. Not women, creatures or plants. He would sleep with a woman if she desired it; he would wash the horses and tend the ducks and pigs because it was demanded of him. He would cut the sugarcane and the reeds in the fields with all the other slaves.

But he didn't want to have a relationship with his own heart. Let it beat if it wanted — he wanted to be left alone.

He believed that if everyone stayed where they belonged, things would work out well. Love only caused trouble in the lives of slaves. He was sure of that. He didn't want to take a chance with the boss who considered him one of his toys, anyway.

Immersed in his own thoughts, the old man knew he wasn't being honest. He had tasted love before he swore off it forever.

It was before the master had bought Ulundi from the slave boat, before the master's son was born. Perro Viejo was a young man and Aroni was still alive, telling stories to the younger children.

Among other chores, Perro Viejo washed down the horses in the river. That's how Asunción came into his life.

The morning it happened was no different from any other morning. As usual, the sun floated over the fields at daybreak and the pebbles on the road got stuck between his toes.

Reaching the river, he rolled up his pants and quickly led the horses into the water. Later, he would have to buy food for the noon meal, stack the firewood and carry out other tasks expected of the household slaves. Thinking about all he had to do, he gently began to rub the flanks of the first horse.

The river water was clear and cold. A few minnows swam curiously near his legs. He could see quite a few blue crab and hermit crab holes on the riverbank.

Perro Viejo was scrubbing the horse's head with a cloth when he saw her. She swam toward him, and every once in a while the sun glittered on her dark skin, its rays filtering through the leaves of nearby trees. Short, curly hair framed her forehead and the sides of her face. She had dark, almond-shaped gazelle eyes.

Suddenly, she dove like a fish into the water and quickly emerged near him, splashing and laughing.

Only then did he realize she was stark naked.

Flustered, he got tangled among the horse bridles and tumbled into the river. When he managed to get back up, he was soaked from head to toe. She couldn't stop laughing.

She was the most beautiful girl he had ever seen. He could have watched her forever and ever.

Just then she turned around and swam off downstream.

Without hesitating, he dove back into the river. He splashed wildly in the water, but the girl was already downstream.

Before disappearing around a bend, she raised an arm as if to say goodbye.

"What's your name?" Perro Viejo called out to her.

She laughed again. "Asunción. My name's Asunción!" And her silhouette disappeared into the shadows.

He continued floating in the water, not knowing whether to swim back to shore or follow her.

He finally decided to get out of the water. He

sat on a rock and began weeping, not knowing why.

From that day on, he looked for excuses to go to the river — to wash a horse, go fishing, get freshwater turtles for the fountain the mistress had in the garden. Any excuse for a chance to see Asunción again.

But it was hopeless because she never reappeared.

The Escape

Fifty years later and still thinking of Asunción, Perro Viejo climbed the plantation fence and looked toward the river. A gust of wind struck his head from behind and carried off his cap. Cursing, the old man opened the wooden front gate and started down the path to fetch it.

The sun was going down and the leaves of the trees turned golden in the fading light.

Perro Viejo walked with difficulty. His legs hurt — they had hurt for days. Beira had prepared a poultice of sage and peppergrass for him. But he was so busy with the chickens and the ducks, and opening and closing the wooden gate every few minutes, and planting malanga and okra behind the shack, he'd had no time to apply it.

He would that evening. He would also smear hot ram's fat on his legs and bind up his sore foot with burlap strips.

Perro Viejo walked slowly, lost in thought. He needed a cane, some kind of walking stick to lean on. He'd ask Cumbá to make him one out of linden or timber wood.

Years ago Aroni had told him that timber was the strongest, most resistant wood in the forest.

Aroni made a lot of things up… The gatekeeper remembered her face, which had darkened considerably over time, and her clouded eyes and hair, still black despite her years. How old was she?

Perro Viejo's feet kicked a little clump of weeds, sending butterflies and bumblebees flying away.

Soon the foreman would parcel out the year-end gifts. Last year Perro Viejo had received this red corduroy cap. It was useful, but not during the middle of the day when it was too hot to wear. One night he flung his machete at a snake wiggling across his shack and he cut a hole in his cap. Still, nothing could be thrown out.

Perro Viejo continued to wear the cap, even though it had a huge hole. Bibijagua, Beira's hen, decided to nest in it. And now it had blown away.

The gatekeeper coughed. He spit to the side, distractedly, and went on walking, still mumbling to himself. Maybe this year they'd give him a coat or a large piece of rough cloth to use as a blanket. Often he woke up in the middle of the night shaking from the cold. He was a very old man. Old people carried the cold in their bones.

The gatekeeper remembered Aroni's twisted and cracked fingers, Má Rufina's shakes, Goyo's unsteady steps, Tumba's cane. He had laughed at them when he was a young man, but now he had also become old. He had been strong and nimble, able to leap on a horse in a single bound, or dive to the bottom of the river… Now he was just an old man remembering bygone things.

A dragonfly fluttered near his face. Perro Viejo waved a hand in the air, hobbled three or four more steps and, terrified, came to a dead stop.

He was no longer walking on the sandy path. To one side he saw a dozen large trees casting leafy shadows. On the other side, squash vines grew wildly, completely covering the ground. Morning glories, brickle bushes and weeds grew everywhere. It was so still. You couldn't hear the whinnying or neighing of the horses at the farm.

Where was he? Suddenly something stirred in the brush. Scared, he turned his head just in time to see a scurrying rodent, which glanced at him quickly and disappeared.

He shuddered from head to toe. He had no idea what had just happened.

Slowly, he turned on his heels, his heart skipping a beat. His cap was still on the ground, but hundreds of yards back. He had walked by it without noticing.

Where the hell was he going? Why had he wandered off the path? Where did his old man legs and his slave feet want to take him? What was he thinking of? What was he planning to do? Escape?

The old man felt his shirt sticking to his bony back. He was sweating. Terrified, he began running. He knew what would happen if the foreman or master caught him where he shouldn't be — far from the gate, away from his dingy room, off the property. He was a slave, not a free man who could walk wherever he wanted. He was not the master of his steps or of the road. Even his bones quivering on the cot at night did not belong to him.

With an effort, he got back on the path. Breathing hard, he dragged his bad leg and, cursing his slowness, he begged not to be seen.

The path seemed to be lengthening, however, and delaying his return even more. He was afraid to be caught running away as had happened to

Cumbá, Coco Carabalí and many others.

Perro Viejo recalled the nights he had been chained, the smell of blood and death. The smell of his own fear.

With his arms stretched out before him, he stumbled past his cap. He was out of breath, more dead than alive. When he touched the gnarled wooden gate, he felt he was finally safe.

He pushed open the rickety gate and went inside.

He limped quickly down the narrow path. He no longer felt his leg or the cold sweat that drenched his face and poured down his neck. He hopped over the stones on the path without stopping.

Once he reached his shack, he threw himself, shaking, on the cot. He was home, crying, ashamed of the frightful sensation of feeling free.

Year-end Gift

The foreman rang the bell and everyone gathered in the plantation courtyard. The morning sun was soft, and the barely moving air carried the syrupy smell from the sugar mill.

The foreman's helpers gave the women white sackcloth dresses with huge pockets and brightly colored kerchiefs. The men received thick shirts and trousers for working in the fields. Even the little boys and girls received clothes and slippers.

When everything had been handed out, Perro Viejo still waited in the sun with his hands in the empty pockets of his pants. He lowered his head saying, "Excuse me, Mr. Foreman, but I didn't get a bonus."

The foreman touched the whip to his boots and scowled at the filthy old man.

"I've given out what I had to give out. Go back to your old shack and stop giving me a hard time." The foreman snorted and turned to leave.

"I thought that maybe this year you'd have something for me — " the old man interrupted.

The blow came so fast that he only realized what had happened when blood spread over his face and he couldn't move. He was on the ground with the foreman's boot pressing down on his chest.

The Bundle

The old man winced when Beira touched his wound.

The whip had pierced his skin from his right cheek all the way to the tip of his chin. His face ached, bloody and swollen.

"Sit still," Beira ordered. She smeared a poultice of herbs and plants on the cut.

Perro Viejo whimpered. The sky was slowly darkening. The bell for lights out was about to toll. Footsteps shuffled outside. Someone knocked on the door.

Beira wiped her hands on a cloth and went to open it.

Several men from the farmhouse stood in the shadowy doorway.

Perro Viejo turned his swollen, worried face toward the ashen wall. In the dim candlelight he recognized José Marufina, El Negro, Carlota Pal Tengue, Manuelito, Cumbá and Súyere...

"Here, take this," one of them said, putting a bundle on the table. "This is all we could get you."

"The old man thanks you," Beira broke in, glancing at the gatekeeper's trembling shoulders.

"What's wrong with him?" Súyere asked, somewhat nervously.

"Nothing. He's just got a bit of fever."

"We should go. He needs his rest," Cumbá added, and the men left.

Beira gently closed the door and came back to the table.

"Aren't you going to see what they brought you?" she asked, untying the knot.

"Leave it there!" the old man snapped, some-what rudely. Then his voice softened. "I'll open it tomorrow."

Annoyed, Beira picked up her shawl from the stool.

"I'm off to my own shack," she said, with-drawing into the night.

Perro Viejo turned over onto his back on his cot. In the half-light, the bundle resembled a crouching animal, ready to leap on top of him. He struggled up, feeling his head, huge and swollen like a pumpkin. He brought the candle closer and opened the bundle. There was a large, faded shawl and a coat with frayed elbows folded inside.

The night was colder than ever before, but the old man, wearing the gifts given to him by the farmhands, hardly felt it.

Súyere

"I found your cap the other day," Súyere said, almost apologizing. The old man turned away. He felt ashamed to be seen like this by a young boy, branded like cattle in the corral.

"Where did you find it?"

"Out there," Súyere said, shifting from one foot to the other. His thin, limber body swung from side to side.

Perro Viejo stared down at Súyere's blistered feet.

"What happened to you?"

The bewildered young boy lowered his eyes. "I dropped a bucket of hot water when I was preparing a bath for the master's son."

"You burned yourself," the old man concluded, struggling to get up from the stool. He took the cap from the young boy's hand. "Wait for me here."

He went to the rear of the shack, picked

something up and came back with a wide pan.

Not saying a word, he put the boy's feet in the pan and cleansed them with the sap of the poró-poró tree, which he had been saving for something just like this. The sap performed miracles. It was perfect for curing wounds, getting rid of stomachaches or frightening off evil spirits.

Súyere noticed the old man's trembling hands, but said nothing.

"You'll be fine in no time." Perro Viejo placed gum tree leaves on his feet and bound them up with a burlap strip.

"You shouldn't bother yourself about this, old man, the doctor — "

"That man's no doctor!"

Súyere shrugged. The air in the shack was moist and light, announcing rain. The clouds moved slowly until they darkened the whole sky. Far in the distance, bolts of lightning pierced the horizon. Loud thunder shook the earth.

"It will rain well into the night," the boy said, taking his feet off the old man's knees.

"Wait a second." Perro Viejo went to the rear of his shack again and came back with a couple of ripe custard apples.

Súyere's eyes lit up. He quickly took the apples and hid them under his shirt. He was perhaps eight or nine, skinny and rumpled, but his face was calm and tender. The master had bought him last summer as a birthday gift for his son.

Súyere reached the doorway. Perro Viejo gazed down at his own swollen leg. Since Beira had stopped caring for it, it had gotten worse. He didn't know how to make the poultice that the old woman prepared, which gave him so much relief.

"Go on," the old man said to the boy.

Súyere ran, hopping and skipping down the path, avoiding the rocks and the brambles.

The first raindrops started falling all at once.

Trees, Plants and Flowers

Trunks of every shape, leaves of every color, flowers of every fragrance surrounded the plantation in a tight green cloak.

Perro Viejo was a friend to the trees. He listened to them from his cot. And in the morning he would softly touch their wrinkled trunks full of sap and dew as if greeting each of them one by one.

The old man knew that the wise yagruma trees, which rose over the fence and the front gate, were among the tallest forest trees. Perro Viejo had been taught that by boiling their leaves, pouring the liquid on beeswax and drinking the mixture before bed, you could cure the flu or a chest cold. The trees also sheltered owls and black fire beetles, and their spiny branches were companions to the wind and the rustling.

At the same time he admired the flamboyant trees, the lindens, the banyans and even the gloomy guasima trees, from whose thick branches slaves often hung themselves.

Cedars, palms and hog plum trees grew farther out from the plantation where the foliage thickened, offering shelter to birds and bees.

But down below, plants and flowers — frescura, verbena, cordobán, oregano, spinach, sweet basil and mint; sunflowers, jasmines, roses, licorice, cojobas, rose apples — perfumed the earth.

On the other side of the river, mangoes, guavas, mameys and orange trees grew — all fragrant fruit trees, juicy and tempting, quenching hunger and restlessness.

Slaves often used herbs to cure the body and the soul. They used sage to calm fevers and sores. Wormseed juice got rid of worms in young children's stomachs. The resin from the pitch apple tree helped to heal lash wounds. Women aborted unwanted children with resin from the calabash tree and the liana. The nectar of the milky liana eased the bites of scorpions and other poisonous insects in the fields.

By rubbing the skin of a runaway slave and her infant son with white lilies and espantamuertos flowers, Carlota made the dogs pursuing them lose their scent.

Elogio Malembe's body was washed with star apple leaves before he was buried.

Newborns were bathed in red grape leaves before they were taken to the orphanage.

Farm hands prepared potions from the bone-breaker wood, aralia flowers, caumoa weeds, gracinia herbs, milkweed sprigs, tonguescraper, pinipiniche and Chinese pepper plant to protect against the master's mind, body and soul. This same concoction was also used to keep away the foreman and his whip and the dogs and their fangs — it was supposed to protect them against the life of unhappiness and chores that they endured on the plantation. But the master seemed immune to witchcraft, and the foreman and his dogs were never fooled.

Don Patricio, one of the few good white men Perro Viejo had ever known, was the only one of those people who ever seemed to have died. He had been very rich and gave away his money so that slaves could buy their freedom. He went from plantation to plantation offering money and comfort. Many children were born free thanks to him.

He died of hunger, poor man. One day he was found at the fork of a road, his eyes wide open, his heart still, his arms tangled in squash vines.

The gatekeeper couldn't accept nature's erratic ways. He simply didn't understand them.

With eyes like wrinkled bark, he could see from his shack the proud, solemn ceibas that surrounded the farmhouse and pigsty far beyond the cane fields.

Slaves believed that the ceiba was a sacred tree, the protector of souls and gods, and a reliable tree for offerings and pleas for help.

Perro Viejo didn't pray for a longer life or ask for permission to walk in the shade of the ceibas in the jungle. He didn't wish to ease his spirits with root and herb potions.

He knew that plants couldn't remove the grief he felt. He knew they couldn't return all that he had lost. Neither the magnificent trees in the country nor the seeds that grew in the fertile earth — not even the majestic ceiba which, according to some slaves, God used to climb down to earth each night — could do this. Nothing could bring back what he had lost even before he was born.

His Name

No one could remember his real name.

The master's father had named him Perro Viejo. The name had been pinned on him when he had been much younger than Súyere was now.

Old Aroni, the keeper of tales, told him how it had happened. Perro Viejo had had two names. The old priest had named him Eusebio and his mother had given him an African name that even Aroni could no longer remember.

Days after his birth, his mother went back to work in the fields, cutting cane and clearing the undergrowth with a machete. Perro Viejo was taken to a large room where three or four old slaves took care of the newborns. He was never in her arms again, but whenever a woman walked past, he would sniff the air as if trying to find a lost fragrance.

The master's father thought it was cute how

the infant sniffed at everyone. He said that it reminded him of bloodhounds when they were hungry, or frantically chasing some runaway slave through the forest.

That's why he named him Perro Viejo.

The old man squeezed his eyes so tight they hurt, but he still couldn't remember his name. He tried to recall his mother's face and her cherished fragrance from among all the memories swirling in his head. It was hopeless. So much time had passed and he had endured so much suffering that his tired head seemed to prefer forgetfulness.

Shadows

The old man quickly pulled his cap down tightly to his eyebrows. He locked the rickety door to his hut with a piece of worn cord and hobbled slowly down the path full of rosemary. It led over a gentle hill and ended at the pigsty and the duck and goose hatchery.

The sky was purple and calm, about to be taken over by the stars above the treetops.

Perro Viejo climbed the hill carefully, head lowered as if watching for every stone and weed. He stopped when he reached the top. He was exhausted. He placed one hand on the fence covered with cojobas and scampering lizards. He waited until he had caught his breath. This happened more often now. He felt like his bones were wasting away under his skin — he was as tired or even more tired than any of the slaves who worked in the fields. There were times he forgot messages or faces or he ended up getting lost on the footpaths through the plantation, the same ones he had walked down his entire life.

One night, while eating his usual meal of beef and vegetables, he fell asleep with his spoon in his hand.

Perro Viejo didn't pay much heed to these misfortunes of his mind and body — it was completely normal for someone well over sixty. What was strange was how much he missed Beira. Before, his loneliness seemed natural and normal — part of him, like an arm or a leg.

But since they had come together, his routine had changed. If he didn't see her for a few days, he grew increasingly uneasy. Quite often, he truly missed her.

He liked having her at his side, not saying a word, just hearing her mumbling as she fussed around the fire. A tear rolled out of one of his eyes. The old man touched his swollen cheek. Treated with honey and sap from the linden tree, the wound had begun to heal, but the burning hadn't stopped.

A flock of birds flew up from a nearby tree and zoomed overhead, cackling.

Slowly, the old man went down the other side of the hill. The sun had set and a light rain had fallen. The ground was damp and spongy beneath his feet.

Perro Viejo smiled. As a child he'd made clay pottery and figurines with his skillful, almost magical, hands. Even the oldest slaves admired his dexterity.

Once they asked him to make a deity for the farmhouse door to protect against evil spirits. Perro Viejo had gone to the riverbank to get clay. When he got back to the farmhouse, he mixed it with twigs and pieces of turtle shell. He made a curved figure with an angry face and stony eyes. It had deep cuts on the face and cheeks, and the hands were arched tensely as if about to fire a small copper arrow.

The image terrified the elders. They were certain that he had made Echu Alawana, the god of desperation and misfortune, who used a whip to guide the dead to the other world. He was the same god who allowed the foreman's bloodhounds to tear slaves into shreds and who raised the master's ire against them on the sugar plantation.

Perro Viejo didn't know *that* god or any other god — in fact, he doubted their existence. He believed that dogs attacked slaves because they had been trained to do so and that the master

turned angry with them for the same reason —
he could not love them. He only knew how to
make their lives even more miserable.

It was absurd to blame anyone, especially the
gods, since they lived in the sky and never
showed their faces.

He had only been trying to make a figurine of
a deer hunter — a jungle hunter like the ones old
Aroni had described in her African stories. But
the elders wouldn't believe him.

That very night they destroyed the figurine
and purified the farmhouse with herbs and
strange prayers.

After that, the young Perro Viejo never
touched clay again.

But now, slowly trudging down the hill, the
old man thought that the games time played
with him were strange. As he got older, more and
more faces and names invaded his head. Only
the memory of his mother remained hidden,
covered in a dark, thick fog. Perro Viejo didn't
remember her name or the shape of her face or
the sound of her voice. She was African, this
much old Aroni had told him. But what did that
mean, other than that she came from far away?

For many people, the slaves from Africa were
a mystery. They often committed suicide or died

trying to flee into the jungle. There were a few in the farmhouse. They spoke little to others or not at all, keeping pretty much to themselves.

Years earlier, maybe twenty years back, he had been friends with one of them — Ulundi. He had started the fire that destroyed the sugar warehouse and killed three slaves.

Ulundi was tall and handsome and didn't look like a slave. He had lion eyes and wouldn't lower his head to anyone. They had been friends. Once Ulundi had saved him from drowning in the river. He helped Perro Viejo and protected him in a way no one else did.

When the foreman hung him from a carob tree as a warning to the others, Perro Viejo almost went crazy. For weeks he plotted to avenge Ulundi's death.

He wept when he saw the crows and vultures feeding off his friend's corpse. The birds had come from near and far, covering the body, the carob branches and even the path with their wings. Before taking the path to the cane fields, you had to throw stones to scare them off.

That was when the crows first showed up at the plantation, and they never left. They darkened the bushes with their black feathers, pecked holes in the harvested corn and annoyed travelers with their chatter. A new path to the cane fields had to be cleared.

Strange things started happening. The plantation had its worst harvest ever. Worms and snakes infested the sugar vats. A dead white man was found facedown by the plantation gate. He was missing an arm.

Perro Viejo didn't like thinking of Ulundi. For some odd reason, every time he thought of him he would forget another of his features. Once he visualized his friend's knees, but he couldn't see his feet. Another time he could only remember his muscular torso, his thick arms and his proud head adorned with braids and colored ribbons. The rest of his body had simply vanished from memory and a thick, dense fog took its place — a barrier of smoke that even the air could not penetrate.

The old man didn't want to lose another of Ulundi's features. He didn't want to see a swirl of smoke or feathers in his place, so he stopped thinking about him. At times his thoughts were fiercer than the forest birds and more fiery than the flames that blackened the sugar vats.

He shook his head. With his mind whitewashed of thoughts, he turned into a swampy area. He saw Beira's shack through the night shadows. He had reached his destination.

Even from outside the shack he could feel the sparks of the kindling in the fire inside.

"Beira!" he shouted, banging on the door.

A dull sound reached him through the wall. Cautiously, the old man looked through a crack. There was barely any light inside. A stubby candle gave off a weak glow from inside an empty gourd. He saw a rickety bed covered with bundles and jars on one side of the room and a table laden with baskets of herbs, sticks, fruit and hand-carved ladles on the other.

Suddenly he saw a shadow fly across the room. The old man backed away from the crack, scared, his heart thumping. His legs barely held him up as he stumbled back to the path.

Unaware of the old man's fright, the night continued spreading out over the forest — numerous stars burst over the trees and the humid earth. The shadow was gone now. Only the scent, Beira's scent, hovered around Perro Viejo.

Aísa

"I'm sure it was Bibijagua," said Beira. "That hen flies faster than a passenger pigeon." She stood before him, her hands on her hips and a pile of kindling by her bare feet.

"It's late," the old man answered, looking down the road.

"Stay a while and I'll make you some coffee." Not waiting for an answer, she pushed the door of the shack open and went in. She pulled up a stool. "Sit down."

The old man hesitated, not wanting to enter. He looked nervously into the room through the open doorway. He felt a strange presence inside.

"Someone else is here," he said.

Beira started laughing. She bent down to stoke the fire with her hands.

Perro Viejo had never seen her smile. It made him think he was in the presence of someone quite different, full of flying, vanishing secrets and shadows. The men from the farmhouse might be right in thinking Beira was a devilish monster.

Beira blew on the kindling. The fire began to grow and her face took on a golden tint. Her hair, gathered together in fine, tight braids, made her face younger and thinner than ever. She was beautiful, much too beautiful. Perro Viejo stared at her scar-riddled shoulders.

"How many times have they beaten you?" he asked.

She stopped blowing on the coals and gazed sullenly at him.

"Why do you want to know?"

"I just want to…those scars," the gatekeeper mumbled.

Suddenly he heard a noise from a corner of the room, behind a stack of dishes.

Beira moved away from the fire and went quickly to the door. She grabbed Perro Viejo by the arm, glanced outside and pulled him in.

"No one's here," she said, closing the door, inserting a strong branch to bolt it shut.

"What's going on?" the old man asked.

Beira ignored the question and placed a stiff leather screen in front of the fire. Then she inspected the walls of her shack, wedging cloths and clods of earth into the cracks. She moved her bed, the dishes and the empty pots that were scattered everywhere.

Perro Viejo didn't understand. He watched Beira, agitated and nervous, as she passed by him, appearing and disappearing in the light. He sensed that something powerful was about to occur.

Beira turned to him. Her eyes were wet, her lower lip trembled. "The girl ran away and came to me. I'm hiding her."

"Who?" Perro Viejo said, almost falling over.

"The girl," Beira repeated, glancing at the corner where the baskets stood.

A young girl with an angular, ash-covered face appeared from under the bundles of clothes. She was between ten and twelve years old. Her skin was light and her short hair was like a bird's nest — disheveled and full of corn tassels and leaves.

Like Beira, she was barefoot and wore a white sackcloth dress much too large for her. She stared at the gatekeeper with fearful eyes.

"Come closer. Let this sweet old man have a look at you," said Beira, stretching out an arm. The girl leapt behind her and pressed against her body like a defenseless creature.

Perro Viejo lowered his head and snorted. "What's she doing here?"

Beira stared at him. "She ran away from the La Merced Plantation and I'm — "

"Are you crazy?" the old man interrupted. "You know you can't shelter runaway slaves. She has to go right now."

The gatekeeper limped to the back of the hut where the little girl had been hiding.

There was a hole in the ground. Scattered about were the baskets from the kitchen of the main house that were used to store fruit and vegetables, pieces of frayed rope, huge carob branches, filthy cloths and dirty pots.

"She has to leave!" Perro Viejo repeated, shaking his head. "They'll find her here any minute."

"She's staying!" Biera insisted.

The old man shook his arms in the air. "Beira, she can't stay here. You're risking your life. The La Merced Plantation is nearby. Tomorrow the bloodhounds will be here looking for her."

The little girl started crying. Beira hugged her, awkwardly caressing her hair.

"She's just a kid," she said.

"She's a slave. She has a master!" the old man said, almost shouting.

All at once Beira ripped off the little girl's dress and showed him her back. Several crusty scars extended along her skinny shoulders and ribs. Her flesh was spotted with dark welts and she had been branded with a hot iron near her right shoulder blade.

"Look!" Beira yelled shrilly.

Perro Viejo lowered his eyes. Slowly, he approached the young girl who stood there, crying and sniffling. He covered her with the rags of her dress and tenderly touched her damp cheek.

"What's your name?" he asked.

"Aísa," she answered shyly.

"Do you have a mother?"

"She has no one," Beira interrupted, pulling a clean dress out of another bundle.

"Yes, I do!" Aísa said, her eyes sparkling. "My daddy ran off into the jungle and the master couldn't get him. My daddy's a free man."

Perro Viejo realized she was not as weak as he had initially thought when Beira had helped her out of the corner.

The thin, awkward body was the same. But something inside her had changed.

"I ran off to find him," the girl went on defiantly. "He's all I've got."

"And your mother?"

"She's dead. My brother was born feet first and they couldn't pull him out of her belly."

A long silence followed. Perro Viejo collapsed

on the stool, resting his head in his hands. Beira went to the fire and weakly shifted the coals.

"What a shame," the old man said. "You lost both your mother and brother at the same time."

"He wasn't my brother," Aísa protested. "He was the master's son."

Beira glanced quickly at the old man. "I'm going to help her get to the Colibrí."

"What?" Perro Viejo's eyes nearly popped out of their sockets. "Are you crazy?"

"Cumbá told me — "

"I knew it. That black man has spider webs in his brain," the old man grunted. "That's why he's always being flogged — his flesh is raw from all the beatings. Besides, that place doesn't exist. You'll just end up lost in the jungle."

"Cumbá is a good man, Mister Gatekeeper," Beira answered, as if chewing her words.

"And why are you now calling me 'Mister Gatekeeper'?"

"Sometimes you talk about blacks as if you were a gentleman from the main house," Beira answered through gritted teeth.

The old man stood up. "I'm going back to my shack," he growled, hurt. "I'm too old for such foolishness."

He hobbled quickly to the door.

"Wait a second, Taita." Beira came up to him and put a hand on his injured shoulder. "Let me open it."

The woman was skillful. In one motion, she pulled out the thick branch bolting the door and opened it wide.

Perro Viejo walked brusquely by her and went to the path, not glancing back.

"Taita!"

The gatekeeper kept walking. He was muttering angrily, spitting and cursing the shadows that crowded him on the path. He could have strangled Beira, he hated her so much.

"Taita, wait!"

A few dogs barked in the distance. The old man froze. His heart pounded wildly in his chest. With muscles tense and alert, standing in the pitch of night, he sniffed the air.

The first odor was that of dew-damp earth, then of carob trees and the nearby flowers. These were familiar scents — he'd known these smells since he was a child.

He closed his eyes and breathed deeply. This time he smelled the odor of urine mixed with sweaty clothes. It reeked of trouble and fear — like a machete blade, like a whip. He knew that putrid, foul odor. He had known it as a child, from the time he was knee high.

"It's the foreman's bloodhounds rousing the men to go into the cane fields," he thought.

Grunting loudly, he felt his muscles relax. He was relieved. For a second he had felt panic — for Beira, and also for Aísa. He had heard the dogs and suspected they were coming after her.

"What's wrong, old man?" Beira's voice came toward him out of the darkness.

The gatekeeper was surprised. He hadn't heard her footsteps behind him.

"Nothing," he muttered.

"I want to explain —"

"It doesn't matter —" Perro Viejo cut her short.

"Cumbá and Súyere are coming with us. They'll take us there. I just wanted you to know," Beira insisted.

"But —"

"You can come with us too," she added. Biera walked away before the old man could react.

"Me?" the gatekeeper asked. The wind answered him noisily, shuffling the pods of a nearby flamboyant tree.

The sky began to clear. A rooster crowed in the humid, aromatic morning air.

Perro Viejo picked up his pace. He had been out much too long.

The Master's Gift

Perro Viejo decided not to bang on the carob knocker.

He struggled up the stone staircase. The climb was difficult for his legs because of the height of the steps — he went up ever so slowly, taking a deep breath at each landing.

From the top, a fat slave with dark, glowing skin looked down scornfully at him and his mud-caked sandals.

"Taita, take off your shoes," she ordered.

Perro Viejo ignored her and kept on climbing, leaving footprints on the staircase.

The stairs led to a terrace, taken over by the cobojo's tangled vines. It was nearly three in the afternoon, but the sun's rays weren't strong. All day the sunlight had been weak, almost velvety. A dull, soft wind blew, gently pushing clouds and birds through the air. Still, the heat was unbearable.

The gatekeeper's shirt was glued to his back.

Shame crept up his neck, clouding his eyes and thoughts.

The master of the house had called for him. No one had told him why, and the old man felt very nervous. His muscles were tense. Maybe they already knew in the main house that Beira was hiding a runaway slave, he thought uneasily. Maybe the master would question him about it — after all, he was a caretaker, the gatekeeper. Not a single soul could walk down the road to the plantation house without being seen by his old, nearly blind eyes.

But this time Perro Viejo's senses had failed him. A snot-nosed little slave girl had slipped into the plantation through a hole in the fence and he hadn't even noticed.

The old man tensed his jaw. He wasn't what he had been two years back.

In the late afternoon, when the sun turned everything steamy in the fields, he couldn't keep from falling asleep on a stool or leaning against a solitary leafy yagruma tree. And yet when he went to bed at night, he couldn't sleep. He would prepare a concoction from scarlet passionflower and lime twigs, but it didn't help — he couldn't get the sleep he wanted.

For Perro Viejo, the worst part of the passing

years wasn't old age, which dried up his body and made memories brittle. What bothered him most was the pointlessness of repeating the same old habits — the pain in his bones that kept him from walking as before, the tottering slowness of his steps, and beginning to grow deaf more than five years ago, though he disguised it from everyone.

He reached the top of the stairs and stopped, snorting at the vine shadows. He still had to walk down the corridor. His legs already ached.

He had not been in the main house for years. From his shack, he could see its white walls off in the distance, making him feel strangely safe. He begged whatever there was up in heaven not to have to run into the master.

He still remembered the time during the fire when the master dragged Ulundi by his braids and killed him in front of the others – tying him to the foreman's horse, then hanging him from the carob tree.

Perro Viejo tapped his chest — he still felt the wound of Ulundi's death. If his friend were still alive, he would certainly know how to help Beira and the little girl. Ulundi was intelligent — he could read and write and he thought about things that others didn't.

Perro Viejo, on the other hand, was different. He was just a stupid black man, an old black man whose thoughts had been dyed white.

He glanced back and saw the slave with the glowing skin down on her hands and knees using a damp cloth to wipe off the mud he had tracked in. The gatekeeper laughed. Fortunately, Beira had nothing in common with this woman. Beira would never have cleaned the master's staircase like that.

He didn't want to inform on Beira. He couldn't. He was still a man — despite his age, his injuries, and his feelings being dulled to the point they had almost disappeared. And he would continue being a man until the day he closed his eyes and left this world forever, walking down the dusty road far from the gate.

His mother was from Africa. Aroni used to tell them that in Africa men risked their lives for their wives. Beira wasn't his wife and Aísa was not his daughter, but he would defend them any way he could.

But what if the master flogged him to get him to talk? And what if he ordered the foreman to take away his food and water, just as he had done to Tumba Cerrada?

The old man was not afraid of dying. He was

already used to it. He had seen many slaves die, but he didn't know if he could bear the kind of punishment the foreman meted out.

When he was a young man, he was punished several times. He had borne the blows since he had a strong back and powerful muscles from working. But now…it was different. After the first lash, his bones would turn to dust under his skin.

If he had a choice, he wished that the moment he closed his eyes would be calm and peaceful. He preferred not to have either the foreman or the lords of earth or heaven near him. That was the only way to die in peace.

He walked down the wide corridor of the terrace thinking about his death.

The master of the house was in a corner at the very end of the corridor, where he could feel the breeze. He was stretched out on a red-and-white-speckled hammock, apparently sleeping. Perro Viejo stopped at the proper distance, lowered his eyes and waited.

A few ants ran between his feet. He could hear the roar of the mill in the distance and every once in a while the neighing of a horse or a man shouting.

A few minutes passed. The gatekeeper shifted

his weight from foot to foot. His ankles were cramping. He nervously focused on the master.

He had thick eyelids and thin blue veins all over his face. His skin was almost transparent.

"This man wouldn't last two days in the farm-house," he muttered.

The master's stomach rose and fell rhythmically. His thin, wrinkled hands hung over both sides of the hammock.

The old man waited another few minutes. Then he slowly walked away, back toward the stairs.

"Perro Viejo!"

The sound froze him in place. The master's voice always made him cringe — it was like ice, like burning iron.

"Yes, Master," he said, walking back with his head hanging down.

"Come here. I have something for you."

The old man approached, with his eyes still lowered. Suddenly he tripped against a cloth bag he hadn't seen before.

"Here's this year's gift."

Perro Viejo stood still.

"I know the foreman beat you." The master got up and walked over to a small, low table and served himself a glass of wine from a slender, dark bottle.

"You've been with my family since you were born. You're a loyal black man, and that's why I want to give you a special gift," he said after taking a sip of wine.

Once more, Perro Viejo stared at the average-sized cream-colored bag.

It didn't seem like anything special, but you never knew with white people. One day they gave you your freedom and the next they ordered you killed — no doubt about that.

His master wanted to give him something and he was worried sick about what would come next.

"Take it, it's yours!" he said, going back to his hammock.

Astonished, the old man bent down and picked up the bag, soft like a baby's skin. He pressed it against his chest and forgot all his bad premonitions.

Maybe there'd be a good pair of trousers or a new shirt inside. He had needed new clothes for years. He had no idea how long he had worn the same striped pants, which he kept up with a rope around his waist. And his shirt was in worse shape. He had had to cut off the cuffs, and it was so worn at the shoulders that the sleeves were frayed as if they were gangrenous wounds. Now his arms were exposed and two or three buttons were missing.

He was too old to dress like this. A couple of times he had thrown a jacket over his shoulders when he left his shack. But he had lost it after the June windstorm, on the very day the master gave permission for the drums to be played. Remembering it made him angry. He had just opened the gate for the master's visitors. He was going back to his stool, when boom! The jacket flew off in a gust of wind.

It seemed that everyone wanted to take something from him: the master snatched away his mother; fire took away Aroni, the storyteller; his memory lost Ulundi's features; the wind took away his cap and jacket; and now his life or death — he couldn't be completely sure which — was slowly taking away his feelings.

At this rate he wouldn't be left with anything that would do him any good in the world beyond. Maybe he wouldn't need a thing, given where he would be going.

He tried feeling around in the bag to figure out what was in it. He felt something hard. A pair of shoes? Perro Viejo didn't like wearing them — he wasn't used to shoes. He preferred a pair of soft sandals to take the shape of his deformed feet. And what if it were a leather belt? What a crazy idea, he thought. Slaves weren't allowed to have belts for fear they would use them to hang themselves. Or worse — they might go after the master of the house with them.

They had always feared slaves. The worse they treated them, the more they feared them.

On one occasion — Perro Viejo smiled as he remembered — he had given the master a good scare. It was five years earlier, during the La Paz Plantation uprising.

That night the bells kept ringing to warn the other masters about the revolt. From the front gate they could see the far-off smoke and fires in the cane fields. It was reported that the insurrectionists had killed the master and his wife, the foreman and two of his five helpers, and that fugitives had come down from the mountains to help the slaves kill whites and rape their women. And they wouldn't stop at La Paz, but spread out through the whole region burning, killing and taking all the slaves with them.

The terrified master gave the order that everyone be locked up, even the slaves who had always worked in the main house, and that double locks be put on the farmhouse doors. But he had forgotten the old gatekeeper. When Perro

Viejo appeared in the portico with a torch in his hand, the master almost pissed in his pants right there and then.

Five years later, Perro Viejo could laugh about it. He had felt so powerful, he could have burned all the sugar plantations and all the masters in the region by himself. What was the use of fugitives, machetes or fires in the cane fields? Having suffered all his life, Perro Viejo could have put an end to that sack of fear and transparent skin all by himself. But he didn't.

That night he slept, like the other farmhands, with a chain on his leg. Still, he felt like a free man, as if he had escaped to the liberated zone in the mountains — as if he had slapped and torched his master.

"Get lost!"

The voice snapped him back to reality. He hadn't been prepared.

"What?" he asked, looking the master straight in the face.

His eyes were blue, ice cold. The old man hardly remembered them now. When his master had been a young boy, he hadn't been afraid to look at them. Now it was different. Either way, he had never seen anything in those empty, dead eyes. Even as a child.

"What the hell are you looking at? Get the hell out of here!"

Perro Viejo lowered his eyes to the gift he pressed against his chest. His arms lost strength, and the bag slowly slipped down his chest to the floor.

The master's gaze seemed to be lashing out at him, but he said nothing. The gatekeeper decided this was the right time to run away.

He decided it just like that. He wanted nothing to do with anything the master's hands had touched — the gift was surely cursed. He didn't want it even if it were a pair of pants or a new shirt. Perro Viejo imagined that if he put the clothes on, his body would break out into blisters and air would escape from his lungs. That blue-eyed devil had killed Ulundi and if he found out about Beira and the little girl, he would track them down with his bloodhounds.

The gatekeeper dragged his leg over to the staircase. The woman with glowing skin was still there, down on her knees, scrubbing vigorously. The old man walked by her, erect, tracking mud on the other side of the stairs.

"But Taita!" the woman groaned.

"Taita nothing, dammit!" the old man's eyes flashed at her.

Now that the sun was streaming down against the side of the house, the heat was unbearable. The white sheets hanging to dry on the terrace were like walls or partitions. There was no breeze.

Perro Viejo looked off into the distance. He could see his shack and the front gate. He shuffled toward them.

Party

When he passed the sugar mill, the old man saw the workers and remembered that the drums would roll that night. Maybe that's why the master had been so polite.

Keta, Trinidad and some of the women were raking leaves, while others prepared small baskets of fruit. Hidden from the master and the other whites, Agustín and Miguelito sacrificed roosters and ducks at the foot of Iroko — a hundred-year-old ceiba tree where the souls of slaves murdered on the sugar plantation rested.

Coco Carabalí placed the farmhouse congas in the shade — they'd gotten enough sun during the morning. The heat made the goat skin resistant and deeper in sound.

Years back, the gatekeeper had heard Eulogio Malembe say that Añá was the spirit who lived in the drum and he spoke as the drum sounded.

Perro Viejo had not heard Añá's words, but he

certainly heard his music. And every year on St. John's Day, the slaves' own night, he would join the other sugar-mill workers, drinking and dancing until their legs buckled.

There were so many dances: the Garabato, the Macuta, the Maní. His favorite was the Garabato — the pitchfork, which only men danced, though once in a while a woman would join in. It wasn't a difficult dance, but it required lots of energy and speed. You had to have strong legs and a good sense of rhythm.

The pitchfork was thrown down and picked up without missing a step; it was tossed from one hand to the other and sometimes the dancer would balance it on his head and spin in front of the fire without letting it fall. All the while the drums thundered and the people made a ruckus.

He also liked the Maní — the dance of the peanut. It was like two men fighting. They pretended to strike each other and then pirouetted from one side to the other. Often the dancers ended up with black eyes or much worse. It was a difficult dance — exhausting — a dance for warriors.

Perro Viejo wasn't a great dancer, but his leaps over the burning fire had at one time won him admirers. He didn't jump over the flames because Añá required it or because he wanted to be the bravest farmhand. He did it for Aroni.

Once the old storyteller told him that that's how people from his mother's village amused themselves. Perro Viejo didn't know if she was telling the truth. Because of her habit of going in and out of the world of tales, she sometimes seemed to grow confused, mixing up her imagination with reality or vice versa.

In any case, he could jump. If Aroni was right, it was as if he was going back to his mother and her family each time he leapt.

At first his friends praised his boldness. But after seeing his dazzled eyes, full of the fire that lit up the sugar mill, they claimed he was crazy and moved away from him.

He no longer jumped over the flames. Not because he didn't want to try again or because his legs wouldn't have borne it, but because he didn't believe he would ever go back to Africa. Not now, not ever. Africa had become another of the tall tales that Aroni told. Perhaps such a place didn't even exist and had been cooked up by the old woman's clever mind.

Perro Viejo shook his head. He didn't want to think about fire anymore. His old arm started aching again and his mother's face seemed even more remote.

He hobbled among the slaves, greeting people right and left. He took a sip of firewater with El Negro, Coco Carabalí and the other slaves.

After a while, he looked for Beira. She was preparing the meal and laughing heartily with some other women. She seemed calm, as if she wasn't hiding a fugitive slave, as if she wasn't planning to escape any minute.

He pushed past without looking. But before he turned the corner by the duck hatchery on his way to his hut, she called out to him.

"Viejo!"

He kept on walking, grumbling and spitting toward the bushes.

"Taita, I left what you asked for in your shack — "

The gatekeeper stopped and turned his head. Beira was back with the other women, busily working.

Perro Viejo didn't know what she was talking about. He didn't remember asking for anything. But if it came out of that strange woman's mouth, it must mean something.

What a woman. Tight-lipped, strange. There in the middle of all the commotion, she seemed peaceful and beautiful. The late afternoon sun glowed in her hair and slipped down her fleshy shoulders like water had over Asunción in the river, fifty years back.

The old man realized he would have had a different life if he had met a woman like Beira when he was young. Perhaps he'd have had children or escaped into the mountains to a village where runaway slaves went free. Who knows? Maybe he wouldn't have waited his whole life for the young river girl.

Some kids ran by and shook him out of his reverie. Asunción dove back into the water and Beira continued working busily, taking the pots out of the fire.

"Maybe she left me the potion for my leg," the old man thought, remembering Beira's words.

He was near his shack by the front gate. He was tired, worn out by the heat and all the memories.

If he could, he would slather Beira's ointment on and rest a few minutes on his cot. He had slept very little the night before. His leg felt like a bag of rocks.

He reached his shack and undid the cord that kept the door closed. Inside, a pair of eyes shone from out of the dark.

The Night

"What the hell are you doing here? Who let you in? How did — " His questions got stuck in his throat.

The angry old man quickly hobbled past her, knocking down dishes.

Aísa moved away from the candle the gate-keeper had lit and cringed in a corner. She was afraid of the old man. He was gruff and grumpy.

"Beira told me that — " she tried to explain.

"Damn woman! If they find you here, they'll kill us both. Get out of here! Go on!" said the old man, beside himself.

The little girl sprang from her hideout. She ran to the door and opened it. "Beira said that you were a good man, but I think she's wrong," she said. She glanced from side to side, and rushed out into the darkness.

Perro Viejo stood staring at the half-open door. A cold breeze blew through his shirt. His ribs quivered. What had he done? Was he crazy? Aísa was only a little girl who wouldn't know how to defend herself. Beira had entrusted her to him, but thinking more about his own safety, he had thrown her out to face the night, fear, the bloodhounds and death.

Ulundi wouldn't have done it. He would have stood up to the master, as he had before he died.

The gatekeeper hadn't forgotten Aroni, Mos, the wagon driver, or Micaela, all of whom had died in the sugar warehouse fire. The master had money problems and was selling children to pay his debts. The mothers went insane watching their children leave forever, tied to the sides of wagons on the way to the slave market. Carlota's sons had been sold, so had Angelina's little girl and María Ignacia's youngest sons...

The farmhands were confused and didn't know what to do. Only Ulundi reacted. He walked steadily across to the sugar mill and went into the warehouse where the sugar cane was stored after it had been dried. Minutes later, everything was engulfed in flames.

The foreman and his helpers used whips and shovels to force the slaves inside to try to save part of the harvest. But there was too much fire and smoke.

Mos — skinny, hunchbacked Mos — was the first to die.

Perro Viejo remembered him coughing all night in the silence of the farmhouse. Talking in his sleep, screaming unknown names. Laughing the next morning when he was told about his screams and his nightmares.

Micaela, his wife, died beside him. She was quiet, toothless and hunched, just like him. They were like brother and sister. They had never had children.

Aroni was nowhere near the fire, but she went inside the warehouse on her own. After the foreman and his helpers dragged Ulundi out, half dead, she went through the burning doorway and closed the door. Just then the roof collapsed and everything was engulfed in flames.

The master came down from his house, crazed and possessed, and killed Ulundi. Perro Viejo's friend, however, had triumphed over the master. His name and reputation leapt over the plantation's walls and he became famous throughout the land.

Perro Viejo went outside and listened. The drums were beating near the sugar mill and the wind carried the singing and the crackle of the bonfire all the way to his hut.

He recognized José Marufina's hoarse voice as he sang to the god of fire and war.

He looked up to the sky and saw a falling star. He asked for nothing more. He had never asked for anything that was beyond his two hands.

He grabbed the stick holding the door shut and went down the path as fast as his legs would take him, using the stick as a cane. He was shaking from head to toe. He squinted at the shrubs and shadows, looking for the young girl. She couldn't be too far off. She must be scared to death, not knowing where to hide. Maybe she had already been caught. Perhaps the foreman's bloodhounds had just picked up her scent.

And it was all his fault. He should have protected her, defended her from danger as someone had once protected him. A few years after his encounter with Asunción, he had thrown himself into the river one afternoon in a fit of rage, desperately looking for her reflection in the water.

Ulundi had kept him from drowning. He had jumped in after him and dragged him to shore, saving him from death and madness.

If he had hesitated for a second, Perro Viejo would have been dragged by the current like a rotten branch.

The old man had not only hesitated with

Aísa, he'd been scared. He didn't know why.

It wasn't the first time that a runaway slave had sought refuge on the plantation. On one occasion Luciano, the blacksmith, had hidden three fugitives. And Carlota Palo Tengue had protected a mother and her small son who had escaped. Even Cumbá joined two fugitives and fled the plantation, but they caught him before he reached the free zone.

Perro Viejo had never been able to help others who suffered the way he did. Deep down, he envied Luciano's boldness, the courage of Carlota, Cumbá's stubbornness in doing anything he could to get his freedom. And now when he had had a chance to do something, he had failed. He was ashamed.

He went up the little hill, leaning against the wooden cane. He looked toward the mill. It seemed as if the fire's brilliance had increased. He could hear voices invoking the ancestral spirits. The chorus of slaves was energetic and melodic.

The gatekeeper was sure that the chant traveled far. Negro Marufina's hoarse voice split the night like a sharp knife.

He arrived out of breath at the path leading to Beira's hovel. There was a light inside. He sighed, relieved. Maybe Aísa was hiding out there.

The Foreman

Perro Viejo knocked on the door and it creaked open. No one was inside. A stump of a candle just about to go out shone in one corner.

The room was a mess. Dishes and pots were scattered on the ground, clothes hung from the table and the piles of kindling. Beira's cot was smashed to pieces.

The old man made out a bundle of feathers under a blackened board.

"Bibijagua," he muttered, recognizing Beira's pet bird. He walked rapidly over to the candle.

The hen's wings had been ripped off and its feathers smeared in blood. It was dead.

The old man picked up the hen and carefully placed it on the table.

A gust of wind shut the door and blew out the candle. The old man was in the dark. Suddenly he had the feeling that someone was crowding his back. Frightened, he swung his cane against the shadows and rushed out, stumbling and cursing.

He quickly walked down the path until he reached the point where the land sloped upwards. He glanced back. The wind wasn't blowing hard, but Beira's door kept slamming as if an invisible hand were pushing it.

The gatekeeper walked toward the sugar mill huffing and puffing. He no longer heard the drums though he could see the fires in the field off in the distance.

Perro Viejo stared up at the darkened sky, which seemed almost connected to the earth. Thousands of stars came into view.

A horse neighed from afar. Perro Viejo pricked up his ears and paused on the path to listen.

For long seconds he only heard muffled jungle sounds — a cricket chirping, leaves fluttering, a rodent scurrying along the fence or through the brush.

He was much too tense — perhaps he had imagined the neigh. He thought about Beira and Aísa and his head spun. If something happened to them he would never forgive himself — to be hung from a guásima tree would be his only comfort.

He was about to continue on his way when he

heard another neigh followed by barks. His heart skipped a beat and nearly ripped open his chest.

They were the barks of the foreman's blood-hounds. He was sure of it. He had heard them from his shack hundreds of times before. He was scared stiff. He had seen Severino torn apart by them before his very eyes. He remembered how their jaws had gripped the slave's flesh — a shiver ran through his body.

Perro Viejo started running as best he could toward the shacks where the foreman lived. The fear of what might have happened made his mouth dry and his back and forehead sweaty.

"Oh, my God!" he said to the shadows crossing his path, to the earth his sandals walked on, to the trees that let their branches and murmurs fall over him.

Panting, he dragged himself to the shacks. Beira was there. So was Aísa. And also the foreman.

The young girl's body lay over the horse's back, held in place by the foreman's arm. He was on the horse, trying to pull his whip out of Beira's hands.

Confused and angry, the horse bucked from side to side. The foreman kept digging in his spurs, trying to get the horse to gallop off, but

Beira pulled with so much strength that his feet got tangled. He could barely keep his balance.

"Let go, you black devil!" the foreman shouted, kicking her.

Beira hunched over in pain, but wouldn't let go of the whip.

Suddenly the man released the whip and Beira fell to the ground. Laughing, the foreman kicked the horse and galloped off. He didn't get very far. Something was clinging to his pants and wouldn't let him go. He glanced back and saw the battered and exhausted woman still on the ground. He turned his head to the other side and saw Perro Viejo.

The old man clung desperately to the foreman's leg as if trying to yank it off. Angrily, the foreman dug his spurs into the horse again. It whinnied and, with fire in its eyes, reared up on its hind legs. The foreman grabbed the reins to keep himself from falling and lost his grip on Aísa.

The little girl bounced to the ground like a ball. Still holding on to the foreman's leg, the gatekeeper couldn't fight the pull of the horse and fell to the ground in a cloud of dust raised by its hooves. As Perro Viejo struggled to stand up, Malongo and Cumbá attacked the foreman.

Breathing hard, the old man looked for his cane among the brush. As soon as he found it, he hobbled toward the men. The foreman, screaming and cursing, struggled to free himself from the arms of the slaves.

When Perro Viejo reached them, he delivered a crushing blow to the foreman's head without saying a word. His face immediately began to bleed and his body grew limp.

The gatekeeper stared blankly at the slaves.

"Go back to the farmhouse and gather up everyone who wants to escape! Quickly, it'll soon be daylight!" he ordered.

Cumbá and Malongo stared at each other for a second and then, obeying the old man's order, they hurried off toward the plantation.

It was only then that Perro Viejo heard the barks of the bloodhounds. The cage where they were locked up during the night was still shut, but the dogs, stirred up by the men shouting and making noise, were trying to break out. Quickly he reached the cage, which was shaking from the press of the dogs, and put his cane through the iron bolts. Then he limped back to Beira and helped her up. Her face was bathed in sweat.

"Old man!" she moaned, tearfully. "They killed the girl. They killed her!"

Beira embraced him. After a minute, Perro Viejo pushed her gently away and slowly went over to the little girl's body.

Aísa was lying on her side, her face hidden by the grass. The gatekeeper kneeled down and touched her arm. It was still warm.

Gently, he put his hand on the young girl's chest.

Her heart was beating ever so softly.

"She's alive, Beira! Come here."

The woman bent over Aísa with glowing eyes. Her hands were shaking and there was a fear and sadness on her face that the gatekeeper had never seen before. She had aged in just a few minutes.

Beira caressed Aísa's hair and kissed her face over and over again. Perro Viejo thought that despite her strange ways, Beira would have been a good mother.

He realized just then that he knew nothing of Beira's life. He had seen her arrive on the master's wagon, but he didn't know if the master had bought her from a slave boat or from a nearby ranch. He didn't know her age or where she had gotten those scars on her shoulders. He didn't know if she had had a family or had always lived alone.

She was sobbing over the young girl. The strength the gatekeeper had attributed to her seemed to have left her. She wasn't a witch who put her hands in fire without getting burned, a sorceress who flew over trees or a woman who made the farmhands jittery with her crazy habits. She wasn't weeping just for Aísa, but for herself as well. Perro Viejo felt that the woman's tears rolling down her cheeks marked the end of a journey that had begun many years before.

He wanted to embrace her, rock her in his arms, tell her that despite his fears and his forgetfulness, she could count on him. He wanted her to know that despite his bad leg and annoying ways, he was capable of going to the ends of the earth if she asked him to.

It wasn't that his fears had left him, but the woman's presence had forced him to forget them. Now Beira was about to go on a long journey to freedom. He was sure of it.

The gatekeeper smiled. His heart had betrayed him. For years it had made him believe that it was dead, and now that he was old and running off to God knows where, he discovered that it was all a hoax.

His heart had always been there, hiding, silently making fun of his trembling sack of bones, infusing him with affection for Beira without his realizing it.

It was this affection that made him limp all the way to her house, not the herbal poultice she concocted to cure his leg or the mug of mountain coffee she offered him in the morning. It was this affection that made him plant seeds, repair stools or carry a box of kindling to her kitchen. That tenderness had kept her close to him, in silence, as he watched her come and go during the passing years.

He loved that strange woman. He had loved her from the first time he had seen her.

His heart had known it, but his confused mind wouldn't let him see anything beyond the grief of his own life.

He wanted to tell her everything that his heart had revealed to him, but instead he said, "Stand up, Biera. The farmhands are coming."

The Colibrí

Not everyone came. The old man saw the shadows of Súyere, El Negro, Carlota, Keta, Agustín and some twenty others walking with Cumbá. They were marching quickly, and every once in a while they glanced back as if they were looking for something.

"And the others?" the gatekeeper asked.

"They didn't want to risk it. They're afraid," Malongo answered.

Annoyed, the old man shook his head. He had hoped that the group of slaves willing to escape would be larger. After having suffered so much on the plantation, he didn't think that anything would hold them back.

But he understood, nevertheless. He had also been afraid. He had also been full of doubt at the thought of walking into the jungle, drifting away forever from what was most familiar.

For better or worse, the plantation had been

his world. From the day he was born, he had known the land that he cultivated, the sugarcane fields, the animals, the foreman's whip, the master's contempt and the other farmhands. But now, he just wanted to escape, leave everything behind. Nothing else mattered.

Beyond the plantation fence was the jungle — the unknown, freedom. But first he had to escape the furious pursuit of the ranchers and their bloodhounds. They would have to endure the fear of being caught, ripped apart by the hounds and dragged back to the plantation in a cloud of dust.

Perro Viejo knew that to go into the mountains you had to be strong in body and spirit — not afraid of the night or the leaves that rustled.

You had to know where to find food, how to walk downwind to hide the body's odor and how to recognize the sounds and silences of the jungle. You had to know why birds suddenly stopped chirping and be able to determine how far away a horse and its rider were after hearing the echo of a neigh or a voice.

Many people didn't have the physical or spiritual strength to remain constantly alert. Not only was escape a risk, but surviving in the jungle also had its dangers.

The gatekeeper understood that. He doubted whether he had the strength. If the Colibrí did exist, it was definitely far away, so far away that it would be almost impossible to get there.

Suddenly the ringing of bells in the distance pulled him out of his reverie.

"We have to head out now!" Cumbá said.

Perro Viejo knew what that sound meant. The master of the house was asking for help from the ranchers of nearby plantations. He was telling everyone that his slaves were trying to escape. Soon a posse of men would be pursuing them, with dogs and weapons.

The old man worried about Aísa. She had regained consciousness, but was in no condition for a long, tiring journey.

"She's too weak. She won't survive," he told Beira.

Just then Malongo took the young girl in his powerful arms. "We're all sticking together!"

"Let's go, then! To the Colibrí," Perro Viejo said doggedly. He started walking.

The Jungle

Daybreak hung over the runaway slaves. The mountains were white with fog. Owls hooted from the tops of trees. Hasty steps ran through the brush. There were mysterious silences, paths that lengthened and curved, roads that rose and fell without warning. Wild animals sniffed their tracks. Birds flew off, scared by their quick shadows. Spider webs hanging from branches disintegrated against the fugitives' faces.

It was cold. Cumbá was at the front, pointing out the path, leading them toward the Colibrí. He was followed by El Negro, Casimiro, Agustín, Bienvenido, Boniato, José Marufina, Coco Carabalí and the others. They were sweating and strong. Behind them came the women and Malongo, who carried Aísa in his arms, followed by Súyere and Beira. Farther back, the old man limped along.

He could barely walk. With each step his leg

throbbed. He cursed his slowness in the cold and the dark.

He hadn't seen Cumbá and the others for some time now. He could just make out Beira's dress in front of him, the outline of her body against the jungle brush. She walked along and kept turning back to look for him. She didn't want him to fall behind. She slowed down so he could keep up.

Perro Viejo did everything possible to keep the pace. His heart thumped in his chest. He was dead tired.

Exhaustion parched his throat. He couldn't stop panting. A cold sweat bathed his face and neck. He could hardly bear the cough and phlegm that came from deep inside him.

He knew that any moment he would stop. His body was consumed by a struggle that had been lost from the start.

Still he continued on for Beira's sake. She commanded him to hurry with her frightful stare — commanded him to follow her to freedom, to end up living with her.

In the middle of this confusion, the old man looked up at the sky. It was growing lighter. Behind him the path was calm and deserted, but something threatening swarmed among the stones and the undergrowth.

Perro Viejo stopped. He couldn't go on. He walked another two or three steps and then collapsed heavily into the dust.

Beira saw him fall. She didn't know whether she should go back or continue with Malonga, Aísa and Súyere. The gatekeeper lifted his head and signaled to her to go on ahead, but she hurried over to him.

Nervously, she got down on her knees beside him.

"Old man! Let's go! Get up!" she begged. She grabbed one of his arms and tried to lift him.

"Go on!" he grunted, looking at her with steady eyes.

Beira was bathed in sweat, exhausted. But the gatekeeper thought she looked beautiful, as always.

"Stay with Aísa. I'll catch up with you in a second!"

"Don't leave me alone! Come on, get up!" she repeated.

"I'll see you at the Colibrí. I know where it is," the old man lied. "Go on ahead!"

"No, old man!"

"Damn!" he growled, pushing her away from him. "Get out of here!"

Beira hugged him tight. Then she held his face

between her hands and said, "I'll wait for you there."

"Don't worry, Beira. I'll get there, alive or dead," the old man answered with a smile and he sat up a bit.

"You'd better," she said, and ran to join the others.

When the mist had swallowed up Beira, Perro Viejo fell back on the ground. The dust made him cough, and he remembered his mother. Her face rose up in his mind without warning.

He recognized her by her eyes, by the shape of her dark face, by her full breasts, by that particular smell he had searched for in other women, hoping to find her again.

Yes, it was her. He had spent a lifetime remembering her and it was only at this hour that her face emerged from the emptiness.

"What's my name?" he asked the apparition calming his thoughts. He saw her thick lips moving, but no sound came out. Barking bloodhounds tore up the path.

The gatekeeper's spirit rose up slowly into the air and with an eye on the Colibrí, it entered the jungle.

Glossary

Añá: spirit that lives in the conga drum
Colibrí: literally, a hummingbird, but figuratively, the place
    where slaves can be free
Duendes: spirits in Spanish and Latin American mythology
Echu Alawana: god of desperation and misfortune
Garabato: pitchfork dance
Iroko: name for a hundred-year-old ceiba tree where the
    souls of slaves murdered on the sugar plantation rested
Macuta: kind of dance
Maní: peanut dance
Perro Viejo: Old Dog
St. John's Day: Day of the Slaves
Taita: term of endearment

There are many plants in Cuba that are not found elsewhere
in North America. We have found English equivalents for
some while we have left others in the original Spanish.